Charlotte's Web™

THE MOVIE STORYBOOK

Adapted by Kate Egan

Based on the Motion Picture Screenplay
by Susanna Grant and Karey Kirkpatrick

Based on the book by E. B. White

One warm spring night, twelve-year-old Fern Arable was jolted awake by a thunderstorm. Then a light outside caught her eye. Someone was in the family's barn! Fern jumped up and threw on her raincoat. She had to find out what was going on.

Her father was out there, tending to some brand-new piglets. Ten of them were perfectly healthy, but one was small and weak. Mr. Arable watched the small one struggle for food. Then, with a sigh, he pulled an axe off the wall.

Fern reached her father just in time. "What are you doing?" she cried, startling him. "You're not going to kill it, are you?"

"It's a runt," replied her father. "Now go back to bed."

"This is unfair and unjust!" Fern said. "How can you be so heartless?"

"The sow can't feed it," Mr. Arable explained.

"Then I will!" Fern snatched the runt from her father's arms and hugged it. "I'll feed and care for you," she cooed. She scowled at her father and raced out of the barn.

Mr. Arable shook his head as his spirited daughter disappeared into the rain.

Fern tucked the runt into her bed that night, and in the morning she fed him with a bottle. Soon the two of them were inseparable. Fern sang songs to the pig and read him stories. She pushed him in a baby carriage and even smuggled him into school! She named the pig Wilbur.

Fern's brother, Avery, teased her about Wilbur. But Mr. and Mrs. Arable didn't interfere with Fern's pet, at least not until he started to grow. "He's not a baby anymore," Mr. Arable explained to Fern. "I'm sorry, but it's time for the pig to go."

Fern's lip quivered and her eyes filled with tears. "But I promised Wilbur I'd take care of him," she said. Fern's mother had the perfect solution: Wilbur could live next door at Zuckerman's farm.

Bravely, Fern walked Wilbur down the road to the farm next door, which was run by her uncle Homer.

"You'll be okay," she assured him. "You'll make lots of friends. Just be yourself – they'll love you! And I'll come see you every day." That didn't make Wilbur feel better at all. When Fern left for school, he tried to run after her school bus!

"Pig's out!"

The other animals on the farm were watching. It had been a long time since anyone had tried to escape.

Mr. Zuckerman and his farmhand, Lurvy, lured Wilbur back to the barn with a bucket of slops. The food was good, but it wasn't what Wilbur really wanted. More than anything, he wished that the other animals would talk to him. Instead, they acted as if he didn't exist.

There was a horse, Ike, who ignored Wilbur completely. There were two cows that were always laughing at the jokes they told each other. (Wilbur could only tell them apart by looking at the tufts of hair on their heads – Betsy's was white and Bitsy's was black.) There was a flock of sheep that blindly did whatever Samuel, their leader, told them to do. And there were two geese, Golly and Gussy, who never left their nest as far as Wilbur could tell.

When it rained, Wilbur raced out into the open pen outside the barn. He jumped in the air and crash-landed in the mud! "It really is a lot more fun when you do it with someone," Wilbur told the other animals. But nobody wanted to play.

Finally the geese took pity on him. They filled him in about life on the farm – but they didn't make it sound as great as Fern had. "Ike's breath could peel paint!" confided Golly. "Oh – and the sheep are idiots."

"Mindless," agreed Gussy. "They drive, drive, drive us crazy. They'd follow a leaf off a cliff if it led them there. And those cows . . . all they do is gossip!"

"But – you're all friends, right?" asked Wilbur, confused.

Golly nodded. "Oh, sure!" he said. "Been here together our whole lives."

Wilbur didn't think that just living in the same place was enough to make someone your friend – not the kind of friend he wanted, anyway. But he didn't dare to argue with the geese. He was too desperate for some company.

Wilbur surprised a rat near his trough one day, sneaking away with the best pieces of Wilbur's lunch.

"Hey, you wanna play?" asked Wilbur. It was a worth a try.

The rat blinked for a second, then said, "For so many reasons . . . no. See, I don't play." He ticked off the things he *did* do on his fingers. "I gnaw, I spy, I eat, I hide. Me in a nutshell." He started shoving rotten food into a hole under Wilbur's trough.

"Couldn't you just stay and chat?" Wilbur tried.

"Chat?" the rat repeated. "Gnaw, spy, eat, hide," he reviewed. "Nope. 'Chat' ain't on the list."

The rat's name was Templeton. He talked a lot, but he wasn't exactly friendly. He was only interested in food – especially if it was Wilbur's.

Fern came to visit whenever she could, but Wilbur was still lonely. Before he went to sleep, he shouted out "Good night!" to each of the other animals, hoping that somebody would respond. They *seemed* to hear him, Wilbur figured, but nobody ever bothered to say "Good night" back . . . until one night a voice said, "Please tell me you won't be doing that all night. I'm trying to concentrate." Wilbur wanted to talk, but the voice said, "Go to sleep. We'll chat tomorrow."

Wilbur couldn't wait until sunrise. As soon as a sliver of light appeared above the horizon, he called out, "Would the party who addressed me last night kindly make herself known?"

The same voice said, "Sssshhh! Pipe down and I'll come out." Wilbur couldn't see the creature until it came down on a silky thread and dangled in front of his nose. It was a big grey spider!

The spider cried, "Salutations!"

Wilbur stammered, "Oh, okay, I'll leave."

Then the spider interrupted. "No, Wilbur," she explained. "Salutations is just a fancy way of saying hello."

The spider's name was Charlotte and, like Wilbur, she wasn't very popular around the barn.

When Betsy spotted Charlotte, she shuddered.

"Eeew. Wish she'd go back in."

"They eat their young, you know," Bitsy added.

"Eight spindly-indly legs," Gussy chimed in. "And fangs. Ugh!"

"Spider!" shrieked Ike. "Get it away from me! Get it away!"

The horse was terrified of Charlotte, and all the animals kept their distance. For some reason, though, she didn't bother Wilbur. He thought that Charlotte seemed pretty nice.

Wilbur could talk to Charlotte about anything – their conversations lasted for hours. And that spring she helped him see farm life through new eyes. It wasn't boring or lonely at all – in fact, magical things happened all the time. The days grew warm and long, and new life was everywhere a growing pig could look. When Gussy's eggs hatched, Wilbur could hardly believe his eyes! Then school finished for the summer, and Fern was there to share it all with him. Wilbur felt happy.

One night, though, Fern's brother, Avery, spotted Charlotte and tried to catch her. Wilbur tripped him just as he was about to take Charlotte away in a jar!

Avery's foot landed in the middle of Templeton's lair, right where the rat had stored his prize possession: a rotten egg. When Avery crushed it, the smell was horrendous! All of the animals complained – except Charlotte. She was just grateful to Wilbur for stopping Avery before it was too late.

"Ironic, isn't it?" Templeton asked Charlotte. "He's saving you, and they're saving him for Christmas."

"What's Christmas?" asked Wilbur.

"The day you'll be cured," Templeton said.

"But I'm not sick," Wilbur replied.

Templeton met his eyes evenly. "Oh, I didn't say you were sick," he said, waiting for the other animals to explain. "It's a sad statement when the rat's the most honest guy in the place."

It was up to Charlotte to tell Wilbur the terrible truth: Spring pigs were often killed before the year was out, their meat smoked into hams and bacon.

Wilbur was devastated. "It isn't fair!" he cried. "I love it here. I want to live here forever. I want to see the snow!"

Templeton sneered, but Charlotte made Wilbur a promise. "Whether anyone else sees it or not, you are a breath of fresh air in this dingy place and I will not let them kill you. I'm going to save your life!" she announced.

"How on earth can you possibly do that?" asked Wilbur.

"I don't know," Charlotte admitted. "But I've made you a promise and promises are something I never break. So go to sleep and let me worry about it."

Trusting his friend, Wilbur did as he was told.

While the other animals slept that night, Charlotte hatched her plan and worked alone. Silken strands poured from her spinnerets, and her eight legs seemed to dance as she wove the silk into a magnificent new spider's web.

The next day, Charlotte's web shone in the morning light. In its very centre, she had spun two words: "Some pig."

When Lurvy came with the slops the next morning, he dropped his bucket and froze. He'd never seen anything like it! He ran up to the farmhouse and tried to explain to Mrs. Zuckerman. "There's something in the . . . it's sort of a . . . up in the . . . yeah, corner . . . You just gotta come see this!"

Nobody could explain how words had come to be woven into a web, and soon people were flocking from far and wide to see it.

Charlotte's words made Wilbur stand a little taller. Suddenly he had some new respect around the barn.

The only problem was that people forgot about it all too quickly. And if Wilbur had any hope of surviving till Christmas, Charlotte would need to keep reminding everyone that he was special.

So Charlotte called a meeting of the animals. Nobody liked taking orders from a spider, but Charlotte said, "Wilbur's life is in danger. And what happens to one of us affects us all." The humans could decide to send any one of them off to the smokehouse after Wilbur. The only way to keep it from happening was to stick together.

Charlotte was looking for another word to weave into her web, and it had to be just right. Nobody had any good ideas until Gussy stuttered, "How about terrific, terrific, terrific?" The spider could only fit one 'terrific' into her web – but otherwise it was perfect!

Once again, it seemed like the whole world came to see the web. They came with pencils and cameras, ready to record every bit of news from Zuckerman's farm. Wilbur stood proudly under the web as people snapped his picture. The other animals were proud of him, too.

"This is nice, gotta admit . . ." said Golly, observing Wilbur.

"He looks good, bless his heart," Bitsy agreed.

"I must say, he looks quite smart," Samuel said. "Impressive, even."

Mr. Zuckerman sold lots of berries and corn to all the visitors. He promised Wilbur a nice new bed of clean straw, too – after all, business on the farm was booming!

People were saying that the webs were miracles. Nobody could believe that a spider had made them on her own. Mrs. Arable even wondered if Fern had anything to do with it! She was starting to wish her daughter wouldn't spend quite so much time with the animals.

Fern and the animals were hoping that the webs had changed things for Wilbur. But even they couldn't stop the momentum on the farm as summer gave way to fall. Mr. Zuckerman was busy getting ready for the cold winter ahead. And one day Wilbur and Fern overheard him talking to Lurvy about repairing the smokehouse! In spite of everything Charlotte had done, he still wanted ham for the holidays.

When the animals met again, Wilbur was discouraged. Charlotte was looking for words again, and Wilbur didn't have any suggestions. The only words he had for Charlotte were silly ones, like "smiley" and "pinkish."

Finally Charlotte interrupted him. "Words have power, Wilbur," she said. "They must be chosen carefully if you want them to be effective." She wasn't discouraged at all – and she hadn't given up on saving Wilbur. She had even found somebody new to help!

All of the farm animals were pulling for Wilbur by now . . . all, that is, except one.

"That rat is always drag-drag-dragging in trash with writing on it," Gussy pointed out. "Plenty of words there . . ."

Templeton hated the idea. "No way," he insisted. "Nothing doing. I ain't breaking my back to try and save 'some pig' – no matter how 'terrific' you think the little lunch meat is."

He changed his mind, though, when Charlotte reminded him that there'd be no more tasty treats with Wilbur gone! Suddenly Templeton was willing to pitch in. He rummaged in a pile of newspaper and brought back a tattered magazine cover for Charlotte. And Templeton's trash gave her inspiration.

Nobody knew it yet, but Charlotte was growing old. Weaving webs had once been easy for her, but that night she laboured heavily over each letter. By the time she was done, the spider was exhausted and out of breath. Still, Charlotte was sure she had done her best work this time. On a crisp autumn morning, her new web read "Radiant" – just like the happy pig lying beneath it.

Charlotte's new web reminded Mr. Zuckerman of something – and an idea that Fern had planted in his mind finally bore fruit. Addressing a crowd of onlookers, Mr. Zuckerman said, "Folks, I want to thank you all for coming. The web says it better than I ever could – he's some terrific, radiant pig all right. Which is why I've decided to take Wilbur to the County Fair!" Mr. Zuckerman hadn't been to the fair in years. But if his miracle pig brought home a blue ribbon, well, maybe he'd spare him from the smokehouse.

"Did you hear that?" Gussy cried. "He's saved, saved, saved! We did it!"

The animals were proud of themselves – and of their good friends Charlotte and Wilbur. They felt certain that Mr. Zuckerman would never kill a pig who'd won a blue ribbon at the fair.

It seemed like a long time since Wilbur had been brand-new in the barn. Now the humans were helping him as much as the animals were. Lurvy gave him extra slops to fatten him up, and Mrs. Zuckerman gave him a buttermilk bath! Everybody wanted Wilbur to get first prize. He still wasn't totally confident, though.

"Have you ever been to a fair?" Wilbur asked Charlotte nervously.

"No," said the spider. "You'll have to tell me all about it when you come back."

Wilbur was confused. "What do you mean?" he asked. "You'll be there, won't you?"

"I'm afraid not," Charlotte replied. "I have work to do. Work that has nothing to do with you. Work I must do alone."

"But – I can't go without you," Wilbur stumbled.

"You'll be fine without me, Wilbur. I wouldn't send you out there alone if I had any doubts," said Charlotte soothingly.

Wilbur had no choice but to trust her. He knew Charlotte would never let him down.

There was only one problem. Just before Wilbur left, Charlotte discovered that Mr. Zuckerman would treat Wilbur just like any other pig if he failed to win. Her friend would be gone long before the first snow fell – and she wouldn't have lived up to her promise.

Summoning up her strength, Charlotte scuttled into Wilbur's crate so she could stay by his side.

"Templeton," she called. "I'll need you to go with me. We'll have to find another word – a really good one."

"Sorry, lady," said the rat. "No can do. My word-fetching days are over. Comes a time when the rat's gotta ask himself, what's in it for the rat?"

Charlotte wasn't in the mood to argue – and luckily she didn't have to. The other animals knew how to convince him. Once they'd been afraid of Charlotte, but now they were on her side. Working for Wilbur had brought them all together.

"I've been to the fair," said Betsy.

"Greasy bits of food all over the place," Bitsy added.

"It's a mess, mess, mess," Gussy said. "Popcorn, mouldy cheese, half-eaten sandwiches, and sticky, sticky, sticky toffee apples . . ."

Templeton didn't need to hear another word. He dived into the crate just as Lurvy shut the door.

The fair was like nothing the animals had ever seen before. On an ordinary patch of farmland, a bustling village had sprung up for the week, filled with throngs of happy people and lit with sparkling lights. There were rides for the kids and games for their parents, with ice cream and toffee apples for all. Cheerful music floated over to the barn as Wilbur watched the passers-by.

His friends thought he had a good chance of winning. He was big and strong now – plus he was famous, too! But Wilbur knew there was a huge pig named Uncle in the pen next to his, bigger and stronger than he could ever be. He wasn't sure he could measure up to Uncle . . . and he knew what would happen if he didn't.

To make matters worse, Wilbur could see Fern in the distance, on the Ferris wheel with a boy. He remembered that Fern's mother wanted her to play with kids her own age, and maybe she was right. Fern didn't need to be hanging around with animals all the time. She'd stayed by his side as long as he needed her, but now Wilbur had other friends he could lean on. Still, he would always be grateful to her. Fern had saved his life when it had hardly begun!

Thankfully, though, he still had Charlotte by his side. Templeton had searched all day for a new word. Wilbur asked, "Is it a good one?"

Charlotte murmured, "It's better than good. It's perfect." Charlotte soothed him with a lullaby, and soon Wilbur was sound asleep. His life was in her hands.

In the morning, a splendid new web was stretched above him. This one said, "Humble."

Wilbur wasn't sure if he liked it. "Is it the right word?" he asked Charlotte. "Is it true? Because I don't really feel I deserve any of the things you've written about me."

Smiling, Charlotte reassured him. "Then it is the perfect word," she said.

After he thanked her, Wilbur noticed Charlotte was sitting on something round and white. It looked like it was made of spun sugar. This was Charlotte's other project, which she proudly called her "magnum opus" – her great work. The sac was full of her eggs!

In the spring, she told him, five hundred and fourteen baby spiders would hatch. Wilbur couldn't wait to meet them.

But first he had to face some bad news: As soon as the fair opened for the day, a blue ribbon appeared . . . on Uncle's pen.

The judging had happened before anyone had seen the web. And so, for the first time, Charlotte's words had failed to work their magic. Wilbur wouldn't be leaving the fair with a prize after all. He'd go home to Zuckerman's farm . . . but not for much longer. It was almost more than he – or anyone else – could bear. Fern started to cry.

"We gave it our best shot, huh?" said Mr. Zuckerman, fighting back tears. "Go get the truck," he told Lurvy. "Let's bring him home."

But just as the Zuckermans and the Arables were ready to leave, the fairgoers spotted the miraculous web. And soon the fair officials realized that they had more than one prize pig on their hands this year! Later that day, the fair officials awarded Mr. Zuckerman – and Wilbur – a special prize. "A cheque for one hundred dollars," said the announcer, "and this handsome medal, a token of our amazement and our appreciation."

The medal was heavy around Wilbur's neck, but nothing could weigh him down now. He would return to the barn to see many more springs and summers, falls and winters . . . all thanks to Charlotte.

Wilbur had everything he had ever wanted: good friends, a happy home, and a long life stretching out before him.

"Won't it be great to be back home again?" Wilbur asked Charlotte, rejoicing. He couldn't wait to tell the other animals what had happened – after all, it was their victory, too.

But suddenly Charlotte's voice was small and weak. "I won't be going back to the barn, Wilbur," she said. "I'm languishing."

Since Charlotte loved big words, Wilbur didn't understand her at first. But Charlotte was dying. She couldn't even climb back into the crate.

"You *can't* die!" Wilbur cried. "Not now! Not here!" After all she had done for him, he would stop at nothing for her.

But there was nothing to be done. "I can die, and I will," insisted Charlotte. She had taught Wilbur so much about the world, but this was her most difficult lesson of all: the natural cycle of life. She would go, but Wilbur would be left to carry her memory – and all she had taught him – in his heart.

"I just. . . I just can't imagine living without you," Wilbur stuttered. "Isn't there *anything* I can do for you?"

The spider smiled. "Oh, Wilbur," she whispered. "Don't you know you already have? You made me your friend. And in doing so, you made a spider beautiful to everyone in that barn. My webs were no miracle. I was only describing what I saw. The miracle . . . is you."

Soon the Zuckermans' truck was rumbling, and it was time for Wilbur to leave. Somehow, he had convinced Templeton to detach Charlotte's egg sac. The rat dropped it to him, and Wilbur carried it back to his crate as carefully as he could. Then Lurvy lifted the crate into the truck, and it pulled away from the barn. Charlotte said, "Good-bye, my sweet Wilbur," and Wilbur watched her, crying, until the truck turned a corner and the fairground was out of sight. He couldn't speak with the egg sac in his mouth but he let out the saddest squeal of his life, knowing he wouldn't see Charlotte again.

Wilbur's life would feel empty without his friend – he owed her everything he had.

Wilbur returned to the farm with his shiny new medal around his neck. The other animals were ready to celebrate – but they could tell at once that something was wrong. Wilbur glanced at the tattered remains of Charlotte's last web, and dropped his head in sorrow. When the animals followed his eyes, they understood what had happened. Together with Wilbur, they bowed their heads in sorrow.

That Christmas, the spring pig saw his first snowfall. He even caught a snowflake on his tongue! It was another miracle of Charlotte's making. Wilbur was full of joy – but also full of purpose. He was preparing to care for Charlotte's five hundred and fourteen children just as she had cared for him. And now finally, as true friends and family, so would all the other animals in the barn.

Wilbur and the other animals took turns sitting with Charlotte's egg sac, and then, one day in spring, it burst wide open! Wilbur was delighted with the baby spiders . . . until they lined up on a fence and began to fly away!

"Good-bye! Good-bye!" they called out, one by one. Wilbur was very sad. It was part of the natural way of spiders, as Charlotte might have said, but he was bitterly disappointed. He had wanted to tell the babies all about their extraordinary mother. He had wanted to pass on Charlotte's love to them. He felt like he was losing his best friend all over again.

Then, from the top of the doorway where Charlotte used to live, three small voices said, "Salutations!" To Wilbur's relief, a few of the spiders would stay.

"This was your mother's hallowed doorway," he told Charlotte's daughters. "She was loyal, brilliant, beautiful, and she was my friend. I will treasure her memory forever. So to you, her daughters, I pledge my friendship forever."

A spring pig – a runt, no less – surrounded by friends, was welcoming his second spring. And all because he saw what no one else was able to see: the grace, beauty and remarkable talent of a common grey spider. It is not often that someone comes along who is a true friend and a great wordsmith. Charlotte was both.